IT'S A PUMPKIN!

Wendy McClure

illustrated by
Kate Kronreif

Albert Whitman & Company
Chicago, Illinois

For Christina, Jon, Andrea, Sue, and Madison,
and also Carolyn, Aphee, Valerie, and Rick.
The party goes on!—WM

For Matilda, Poppy, and Emery,
with love—KK

Library of Congress Cataloging-in-Publication data is on file with the publisher.
Text copyright © 2020 by Wendy McClure
Illustrations copyright © 2020 by Albert Whitman & Company
Illustrations by Kate Kronreif
First published in the United States of America in 2020 by Albert Whitman & Company
ISBN 978-0-8075-1216-6 (hardcover)
ISBN 978-0-8075-1217-3 (ebook)
Printed in China
10 9 8 7 6 5 4 3 2 1 RRD 24 23 22 21 20

Design by Aphelandra Messer

For more information about Albert Whitman & Company,
visit our website at www.albertwhitman.com.

They found it in the
middle of the road.

"What is it?" Field Mouse asked. "It looks kind of familiar."

"I don't know," said Squirrel. "It's a mystery."

"I'll tell you what it is," said Field Mouse.

"It's in the way."

They pushed it over so that it could roll.

It rolled and rolled...

all the way to the
opossum's nap spot.

BONK!

"Sorry," said Field Mouse.

"What is it?" Opossum asked.

"That's just what we were wondering," said Squirrel.

Opossum squinted at it. Then he sat on it.

"Hmm," he said. "It's a chair."

They all tried it.

"Pretty comfy," said Opossum.

"Disagree," said Squirrel.

"I don't think it's a chair,"
said Field Mouse.

"Of *course* it's not a chair," called the raccoon from her window.

"So what is it?" asked Opossum.

"Is it for eating?" guessed Squirrel.

"Well, now that you mention it..." said Raccoon. "Wait right there!"

A moment later, she came out with a big plate of cookies.

"Get up from that chair," she told Opossum.

"I thought you said it wasn't a chair," he said.

"It's not!" Raccoon set the plate on top.

"See?" she said. "It's a table."

"A table!" said Field Mouse.
"Are you sure?"

"Please have some cookies," said
Raccoon. "I made way too many."

Opossum went to get cider.

The rabbit family joined
them, and the woodchuck
too, and the party started.

"This is fun," said Woodchuck. "But...you call that a *table*?"

"Actually," said Squirrel, "we don't know *what* it is."

"I know one thing we can do with it," said Woodchuck. "Come on."

Woodchuck set it next to the door to his burrow.

"See?" he said. "It makes a nice doorstop."

They carried the cookies and the cider through the open door, and the party went on.

The chipmunk stopped by,
and even three chickadees.

"This is great," said Squirrel.
"We never have parties!"

Field Mouse was just pouring another cup
of cider when the door went

SLAM!

Everyone turned to see the skunk standing there with a sly smile.

"*Skunk*," said Woodchuck, "why did you move the doorstop?"

"I happen to know," she said, "that it's *not* a doorstop."

"No kidding," said Squirrel. "But what is it?"

"I've seen it at people's houses," replied Skunk.
"It's a lamp."

"A *lamp*!?" said everyone.

"I'll show you," she said. "Who's got a knife
and a big spoon? And we'll need a candle."

It made a very nice lamp.

It had a jolly face, and it flickered, and it made
them all want to dance spooky dances.

The party went on.

"But are you *sure* it's a lamp?"
Field Mouse asked Skunk.
"What if someone..."

"WHOOPS!"
said Woodchuck.

"knocks it over?" finished Field Mouse.

The crowd looked at the broken mess.

"What is it now?" whispered Raccoon.

One of the rabbit twins sniffed at the pieces.

"I think...it could be a pie?" she said. "Like our grandmother used to make?"

"Yes!" said her brother. "A big pie! We can make it."

Everyone helped.

Squirrel sighed after he finished his pie slice.

"Whatever it was," said Squirrel, "it was tasty."

"Don't say *was*," said Chickadee. "It's not all gone yet."

He hopped over to a bowl that Skunk had filled with glop while carving the lamp.

He picked some of the seeds out.

"Oh, I bet it would be delicious to roast those," said Raccoon.

"Let's do it!" said Field Mouse.

"Everyone can take some seeds home," said Woodchuck.

The party was almost over.

They all helped clean up. The rabbits and Skunk did the dishes.

Opossum emptied the glop bowl outside.

Then it was time to go.

Field Mouse ate her seeds all at once.

Squirrel stashed his away and savored them slowly over the winter.

Woodchuck slept all winter and saved his seeds for a snack when he woke up.

By spring, everyone had forgotten
about the party and about IT.

They were busy doing other things.

Then one morning Opossum
was scurrying home to bed
when he saw something behind
Woodchuck's burrow.

He called over Field Mouse and Squirrel.

"Look!" he said. "It's a plant."

Everyone watched
it all summer.

"It's a BIG plant,"
said Raccoon.

A few weeks later, Skunk said, "Wow! It's a flower!"

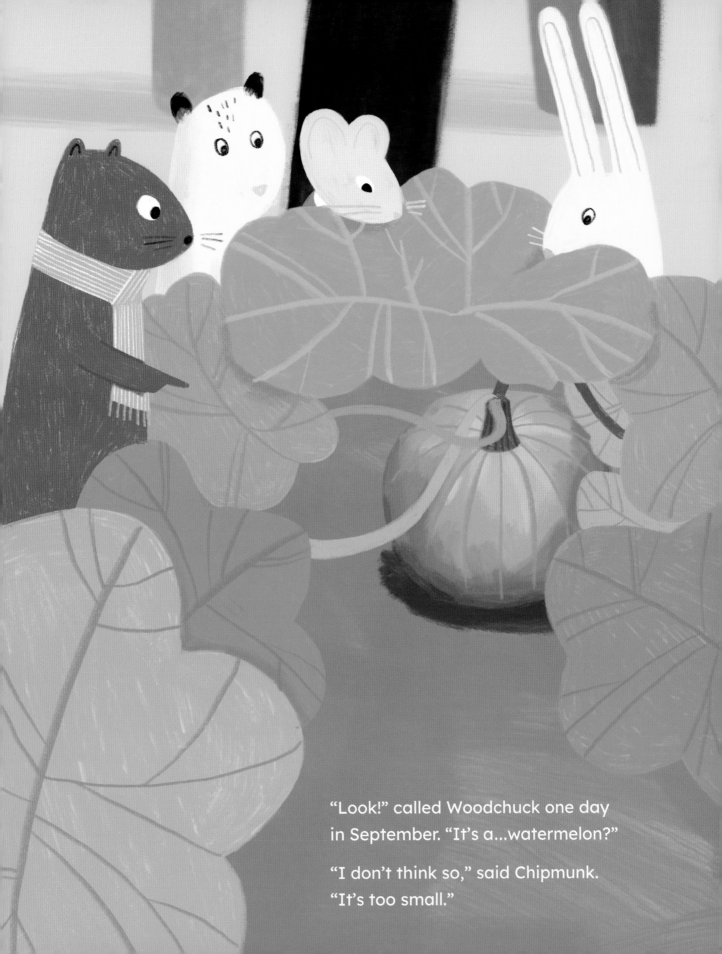

"Look!" called Woodchuck one day in September. "It's a...watermelon?"

"I don't think so," said Chipmunk. "It's too small."

"It's getting bigger," said the rabbits.

"It's getting *orange*!" said Chickadee.

"It looks *very* familiar," said Field Mouse.

"I know what it is!" said Squirrel.

"What?" asked Opossum. "What *is* it?"

"It's time," answered Squirrel.
"It's time for a party."